# PRUDENCE
# of Plymouth Plantation

by
*Colleen Reece*

YOUNG READER'S CHRISTIAN LIBRARY

Illustrations by
*Ken Save*

A BARBOUR BOOK

ISBN 1-55748-674-3

Published by    Barbour and Company, Inc.
                P.O. Box 719
                Uhrichsville, OH 44683

Printed in the United States of America.

95  96  97  98  99  5  4  3  2  1

## NOTE TO READERS

You won't find Prudence or Jamie's name in the list of those who bravely came to America on the *Mayflower*. However, they are real in the sense that they represent the boys, girls and teens, along with their parents, who sought a home in a New World, and were willing to endure great hardship in order to worship God as they felt led to do. No price could be higher than the religious persecution they faced for their beliefs while living in England at that time.

Also real is the daily life shown in this story and many actual historical persons such as Squanto and Massasoit, the friendly Indians; Governor Bradford; Myles Standish; and others who sacrificed so much in the founding of our country.

" TALKING TO YOURSELF AGAIN, PRUE ? "

# 1
## *Adventure Ahead*

Fifteen-year-old Prudence Simmons snapped the last wet sheet and hung it so the frisky summer breeze would blow it dry. "There. Dance in the wind. The next time you get washed it will be—"

"Talking to yourself again, Prue?" A teasing, boyish voice asked.

She whipped around so fast that her flaxen hair tore free from its moorings and swirled across her tip-tilted, freckled nose, and accusing blue eyes. "Jamie Lowe, if you creep up behind me one more time I'll pound you." She stared at the tall lad who grinned at her with mischief in his dark eyes. Jamie's eyes matched his close-cropped hair; he wore a round cap that identified him as a fisherman.

"Don't be mad. I just stopped by to see how your packing was coming. Anything I can do to help?"

She looked down so he wouldn't see the tears she felt rushing to her eyes. "Yes. Convince Father and Mother not to leave Holland."

"Prudence Simmons, you're an ungrateful girl! Going to America is the best thing that ever happened to us."

Stung by his scornful words, her tears dried. "All we do is move, move, move," she cried. "First, we leave Scrooby, England, where Elder Brewster set up our secret church so we could worship God for ourselves and not the way the King and Queen told us to. Then, we sail for Holland—"

Again Jamie interrupted. "Come on, Prue. That was way back in 1608. You were only three years old. How much can you remember? I was five, and all I remember is crossing the water."

"I remember living in Amsterdam before moving to Leyden," she told him, and put her hands on her hips. "No one persecuted us there because we are Separatists. I loved it there."

"COME ON, PRUE. THAT WAS WAY BACK IN 1608."

"I did, too." Jamie sighed.

Prudence saw his face cloud over. "I know we had to leave England," she admitted. "It's a good place for rich people, but poor folks like us could barely scratch out a living. Besides, some of our people were put into gaol* for speaking out against the Church of England. We even had to slip away in the dark of night."

The cloud over Jamie's face blackened, and his strong hands, tanned by long hours in his father's fishing boat, clenched. "King James said that he ruled by divine right and that kings are God's lieutenants who sit on God's throne. Anyone who spoke out against his decree was called a nonconformist, and some of our leaders were even hanged on the gallows."

"I know all that, Jamie," Prudence said in a small voice. She hated quarreling with the young man who had been her neighbor and best friend since childhood. "I just don't see why we have to leave Holland. Oh, I've heard our parents talk. They aren't allowed to buy

---

*jail

"I JUST DON'T SEE WHY WE HAVE TO LEAVE HOLLAND."

land or hold skilled jobs here, and they are afraid for their children." She smiled. "The Dutch are so joyous, always dancing and laughing—even on Sundays." She made a face. "*We* spend Sundays in church wishing we could be outdoors playing with the children from Holland." Her ears tingled when she thought how the deaconess boxed them for talking or laughing in church. Once, Jamie had been whipped with a birch rod for grinning during the lengthy sermon.

"Elder Brewster fears we'll give up our beliefs, and some have," Jamie reminded. "My own older brothers have married Dutch girls and refuse to leave Holland now that Father has decided to go." He looked serious. "Once we get to a new land, we'll be free, Prue. Truly free. There's land waiting and streams and forests with fish and game." A dreaming look came into his eyes. "We'll have a good life." His smile made Prue feel better. So did his quiet reply: "I won't let anything harm you. Haven't I always taken care of you?"

"Y-yes. But they say there are Indians and wild ani-

"WE'LL BE FREE, PRUE. TRULY FREE."

mals in the New Land," she faltered, although her heart beat fast at the new look that had crept into her playmate's eyes.

"A man can settle in and think about taking a wife," he told her. "There's land aplenty for building houses."

Prue blushed. Even though she sometimes thought about the fact that she and Jamie were no longer children, marriage seemed a long way off; in spite of the fact that many of their friends, some even younger than they, had already wed.

"Captain John Smith says the New World is a wonderful place." Excitement filled Jamie's face. "The soil is fertile. And the coast fishing! Why, fish are so abundant you can catch them with nets. Trading in furs is becoming profitable, too, but I'll stick with fishing. I don't like seeing things killed."

"Neither do I." Prue's mind turned to other things. "Many of our older people refuse to go. Hunger and sickness and lack of water took 130 lives at sea on a recent voyage."

"THE NEW WORLD IS A WONDERFUL PLACE."

"Ours will be different," Jamie comforted. "Elder Brewster and William Bradford and the others will see to that. Didn't Robert Cushman and John Carver go straight to the king and get a grant of land in the New World?" His cheeks flushed with red.

"And didn't God help us by causing wealthy merchants to give us money for the trip? Prue, never forget—we're going to America so we can have a settlement where we can worship Him and read the Bible for ourselves." He took a deep breath and his eyes shone. "Just think, forty-one of us—more than half of whom are children—are making this voyage, along with sixty-one Strangers*." His voice deepened. "The next voyage may bring a hundred or more. Never in history has a small group of persons had the chance to set forth on such a glorious adventure! Elder Bradford says when we sail from Holland, we will be pilgrims. Pilgrims for our Lord; who could ask for anything better? Jesus Himself had no

---

*Other English people who made the voyage sought a better way of life, although not for religious reasons.

"JESUS HIMSELF HAD NO HOME."

home once He began His preaching. Are we better than our Master?"

Tears of sympathy and regret choked off Prudence's voice, and her companion's ringing words touched her tender heart. She held out both hands. "I'm glad you are my friend."

He took her hands in his and smiled. "So am I." The next moment he freed her, tossed his cap in the air, and whooped. "New World, we're coming! Get ready for us!"

Prudence watched him run down the lane toward his own home. How sturdy he had grown! How sure he was of himself, and that this journey was according to God's will. Her own heart caught fire at the thought. Did no the Bible say, *"The Lord is on my side; I will not fear..."* (Psalm 118:6)

"Dear Father, be with us and help me not to be afraid," she prayed. A merry breeze cooled her hot face, and she turned back to her work, glad the sheets had dried. Much remained to do before they sailed.

HOW STURDY HE HAD GROWN.

Prudence had need of all her renewed faith and courage in the days remaining. Her younger sisters, Charity and Abigail, trotted after her, asking a thousand questions.

"Will Grandfather go?"

"Do Indians really steal children?"

"Will we have to go naked and not have any clothes?"

"How far is the New World?"

"Will we be hungry?"

She tried to answer their questions and soothe their fears as Jamie had done for her, but the rumors older people talked about in front of the children did little to help. Those who had gone back on their promise to sail, did everything they could to discourage the voyagers. By the time two ships, the *Speedwell* and the *Mayflower*—which was much larger—had been chartered, Prue felt numb. She shuddered at tales of disease-carrying bugs and rats and sighed with relief when both ships were scrubbed down. The *Mayflower's* former cargo had been wine, so its occupants wouldn't have to

PRUE FELT NUMB.

put up with foul smells from the cargo, especially fish. The *Speedwell* was overhauled, repaired, and given taller masts and larger sails so she would be able to keep up with the stronger *Mayflower*.

❖

August 1, 1620, dawned as thick with mist as Prudence's overflowing heart. Would she and the others ever see family members left behind again until they reached the heavenly shore? Prue's arms tightened about Abigail and Charity's shoulders when she saw weeping Dorothy Bradford turn from her little son, John, who was to be left in the care of another family so she could join her husband William on the *Speedwell*. How could she do it? At least, the Simmons family would face whatever lay ahead together: Father, Mother, their three girls, and Grandfather. A final prayer, last embraces, brokenhearted waving, and the ship began to move, on her way to Southampton, England.

Five days later, the *Speedwell* dropped anchor next to the *Mayflower*, which was three times her size and

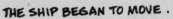
THE SHIP BEGAN TO MOVE.

was carrying the London Strangers. Prudence felt her heart pound at the eager way the two groups met. A pang went through her at sight of the nearby neat cottages, but she resolutely turned away, feeling odd and drab in her dark, hooded cloak which she wore over a long-sleeved dark green gown with plain linen cuffs and large collar, and which covered her from head to toe.

How different the Strangers looked! Although poor, they wore vivid colors with lace, buttons, braid, and feather trimmings.

"See the shore man?" Round-eyed Abigail tugged at her sister's arm.

"Shhh." Yet Prudence's eyes opened wide at the flaming-haired, red-faced, mean-looking Stranger someone called Myles Standish. His wife, Rose, stood nearby, along with the Mullins, a strong young man named John Alden, and others Prue knew would become as familiar as her family during the long journey. She turned toward Jamie and his father. The look in their faces kept her from speaking. Mrs. Lowe had died some time

A MEAN LOOKING STRANGER CALLED MYLES STANDISH.

before. Of his sons, only Jamie would accompany Mr. Lowe to the New World. Yet, they turned their gaze westward, faith and hope shining in their dark eyes, and eager to be off.

A week passed while the *Speedwell*, which leaked, was recaulked, and the business sponsors argued with the Separatists and demanded ownership of the colonists' homes to be built. Finally, the ships sailed. William Brewster, in hiding from the police, slipped past them and boarded the *Speedwell*, to his little band's delight. The ship had been offset by stormy weather that proved it unseaworthy. Another delay, another try. Three hundred miles westward, the *Speedwell's* leaking grew dangerous. They put back to land, the *Mayflower* accompanying them to Plymouth, where the smaller ship was pronounced unfit for ocean travel!

For seven weeks passengers had been ill, haunted by too little food and fresh water. September was half over, and with it, hopes for putting in crops for autumn harvest. Leyden emigrants transferred to the *Mayflower*.

PASSENGERS HAD BEEN ILL.

Some gave up the idea, along with some of the London group. Yet singing, praying, and facing toward the New World, Prudence and her family, the Lowes, and the bravest of the Separatists settled into their uncomfortable quarters for the long, frightening journey across a vast, tossing ocean.

THE LONG FRIGHTENING JOURNEY.

"I NEED YOU, PRUE."

# 2
## *Tall Sails, Tall Tales*

"If it weren't for Jamie, I don't think I could bear it," Prudence whispered to herself and clutched the railing of the heaving *Mayflower*. Gray, gray, gray surrounded her. Clouds, sea, and her spirits—all the same drab color. The long delay because of the crippled *Speedwell* had taken its toll. Why, the time they'd lost because of her would have taken them nearly to the New World!

"I need you, Prue." Mother's reminding voice cut into the girl's thoughts. Prudence sighed. Someone always needed her, what with so much sea-sickness. Those who escaped cared for those who did not. Prue learned to rejoice when fair skies and good winds came. They gave her a chance to slip on deck for a time, or get some much needed rest from the continual fight to keep clean. How she longed for land, a precious place away from the confinement of life on board a ship! Storms terrified her, even more after John Howland was thrown into the sea. Thank God he'd held on to the top-sail halyards* until he could be hauled aboard.

She loved early evening best, when sunset painted the waters rose and gold. With the day's work put aside for a time, the little group gathered, prayed, sang hymns, and talked about their new homeland.

"Just so we don't end up like the Lost Colony," a weathered traveler commented.

"Tell us about it," Jamie pleaded, face aglow. He sat crosslegged on the deck next to Prue, who leaned against a heavy barrel.

The old man's lips settled into a grin. He often said nothing on earth was better than tall sails and tall tales. "Lemmee see, 1585, it was, that Sir Walter Raleigh sent a band of men—'bout a hundred—to settle in the region called Virginny.** They dug in on Roanoke Island off shore but had a mighty thin time of it." He stopped

---

*ropes for raising/lowering sails
**Virginia

THE OLD MAN'S LIPS SETTLED INTO A GRIN.

to puff on a disreputable pipe. "'Long about a year later, they sailed back to England and more colonists came, with supplies 'n such. Most of them also went back—all 'cept fifteen, 'tis said.

"In 1587, 'nother bunch came, this time with a women 'n children. The sailors dumped them on Roanoke but they couldn't find nary of the fifteen that stayed."

"What happened to them?" Prue burst out.

"Now, that's plumb curi's." A hint of mystery came to the storyteller's face. "But things get curi'ser. 'Bout a month after the new bunch came, the first English child was born. Virginny Dare, they called her, John White's granddaughter. He went back to England for supplies, badly needed. 'Long comes the Spanish war, and White can't get back 'til 1591."

Prue's nerves screamed as he pulled on his pipe. He finally said, "When White landed, he couldn't find hide nor hair of those colonists! All he found was the letters CRO carved on a tree and the word *Croatan* on another."

"Really?" Jamie's head snapped back. "How could

"WHAT HAPPENED TO THEM?"

more than 100 settlers just vanish?"

"I said it was curi's, didn't I?" The old man's eyes twinkled. "Some folks 'lowed that they'd been captured by hostile Injuns. Others figgered they coulda joined a tribe called *Croatans* or gone off with friendly Injuns to find food. Anyhow, they'd disappeared, even little Virginny Dare. Nobody's ever known how, or why, and I reckon they never will."

Prudence pulled her shawl closer around her and shivered. What kind of country lay ahead, a land that could swallow a whole settlement and leave no trace?

Jamie glanced at her and smiled. His steady, dark eyes reminded her better than words of his promise to take care of her. He'd been just wonderful on the uncomfortable voyage—doing far more than his share in helping to clean up after sick passengers, carry slops, and lend a hand wherever needed. The first month hadn't been so bad, but the mid-ocean storms that had raged had forced open seams and cracked one of the main beams. There had been talk of turning back, but the crew

WHAT KIND OF COUNTRY LAY AHEAD?

had repaired the ship and recaulked her seams.

A mewling cry brought Prue back to the present. Oceanus Hopkins had been born to Elizabeth just days before. Mother had helped but no young girl such as Prudence had been allowed to be present during childbirth. The look on Elizabeth's face when Prue had slipped in to see the new baby haunted her. Although Elizabeth was tired and weak, faith and love had shone in her eyes when she'd looked first at her husband, Steven, then at her little son. "He will grow up free," she'd whispered.

As the *Mayflower* tossed and rolled, it continued to sail on. Now the quantities of vegetables, lemons and limes, hardtack,* flour, potatoes, dried beans, and tubs of butter, bacon slabs, oil, salt, and casks of fresh water dwindled. Small chests filled with personal belongings, bedding, and clothing provided necessities while trinkets to trade with the Indians remained packed, as did tools and guns for defense once they landed.

---

*dried biscuits

"HE WILL GROW UP FREE."

Bibles and other religious books, and Doctor Fuller's medical books also traveled to the New World; so did twelve servants and six orphaned children to help build the colony. Given clothing, food, shelter and passage, the servants signed contracts to serve without freedom for seven long years. They could not marry without their masters' permission and could be sold. Jamie secretly raged to Prue that it seemed horribly unfair, but those who came to be called "indentured servants" were willing to work those seven years in order to be free and in a new land.

One day, a loud explosion sent Prudence running toward the noise. A crewman held a small boy in an iron grip. "Ye limb of Satan! Ye could've sent us all to the fishes." He shook the hapless boy. "Shooting off a musket near a keg of gunpowder? Pah, ye doesn't have a brain in your empty head!" With another shake that rattled the troublemaker's teeth, he flung him to a pile of rope coiled nearby and stalked off. Wails from the far end of the deck, a little later, showed that the grim-faced

"YE COULD'VE SENT US ALL TO THE FISHES!"

father who snatched his son and marched him off was doing all in his power to prevent another such offense.

Nearer and nearer the coast, they sailed. The whole company mourned the death of William Butten on November 6, a young servant, and the only one of the passengers who died on the voyage. Prue stared into the endless sea, cold clear to her bones. Sometimes she wondered if there had ever been anything except the ocean and life aboard ship.

Battered and driven, the ship plowed on. William Bradford, who had come to the Separatists at age seventeen and gone with them to Holland, brooded over his frail wife's discouragement and ill health. Prudence saw how sad she looked and remembered the parting in Holland, with little John being left behind. Sleeping without beds, wearing as many clothes as possible to keep warm, and trying to cook over a tiny pan of coal was hard on everyone, but more so on the weak. So was the monotony of day following weary day.

However, even the worst of times ends. More than

THE SHIP PLOWED ON.

two months after leaving England, the *Mayflower* crew cried out the long-waited-for signal, "Land ho!" when a thin strip of land appeared on the horizon. All who were able rushed to see. Prue and Jamie stood side by side, but Prue couldn't see for the happy tears in her blue eyes. When she wiped them clear, a bleak, sandy shore with a few trees and no buildings appeared. Her heart sank. Where were the wonderful forests filled with game? The fertile soil for growing food? This rocky coast seemed to shout, "Go home."

Silence broken only by a restless wind and the creak of ship timbers hung over the ship.

"I heard the captain say we're a lot farther north than we should be," Jamie said in a low voice. The wind ruffed his dark hair, uncovered when he'd first caught sight of land. "Shoals and winds have forced us away from the original grant of the Virginia Company where we'd agreed to settle."

"What will we do?" she whispered back, noticing her parents' and the others' grim expressions.

"LAND HO!"

"I don't know." He awkwardly patted her arm. "At least our Heavenly Father has brought us across the sea."

Thankfulness filled her. It remained the next day when the *Mayflower* anchored in Provincetown harbor inside the tip of Cape Cod.* At that time, the leaders called the men together. Prue couldn't bear to miss out on what she felt would be something important. She hid herself nearby and listened with all her might.

William Brewster, William Bradford, and others spoke, saying, "You remember how our sponsors demanded that the homes we build would be company property and how they said that we must work seven days a week for them?" Heads nodded, and Prudence burned with anger at the unreasonable demands.

"We refused, and sold our tubs of butter to pay port fees. Now, we must draw up a plan we will abide by to rule ourselves."

One of the men who wasn't a Pilgrim protested. "If you Separatists seize power, you will force us to obey."

---

*in what is now Massachusetts

SHE LISTENED WITH ALL HER MIGHT.

"No," William Brewster said. "We came here for freedom."

Prudence listened even harder. A long time later after the men wrote down then discussed their ideas for a government, they agreed to a plan and signed it.* They would wait for no king to tell them the law, but would pass their own laws and obey them, the first colonists ever to do so. Every man would vote and take part in governing. If he did not do a good job, the group would elect another. They soon chose John Carver, a godly, well-liked man, to be their first governor.

Prudence knew she would never forget the moment. At last, she and her people were truly free of King James and his persecutions.

---

*This agreement came to be known as the *Mayflower Compact.*

"NO... WE CAME HERE FOR FREEDOM."

JAMIE WAS THE FIRST TO STEP FORWARD.

# 3
## Exploring the New World

Amidst the excitement of signing the agreement that would govern the new colonists, another baby was born. Susanna White named her son Peregrine, which means wanderer. Again, Prudence saw the joy on the new mother's face and smiled. One day, she would also be a wife and mother. Jamie stood taller and handsomer each day, but her feelings were changing toward him. More than a childhood playmate now, she found her heart fluttering when he looked her way and smiled.

Yet, not all his mischief had gone. His desire for adventure stayed and when the leaders of the group called for volunteers to go ashore and seek out a goodly place for the permanent settlement, he was first to step forward. Prue's cheeks flushed red with pride at the straight back and soldier-like way he strode after Myles Standish, who had been put in charge as Captain. Fully armed against possible danger, the brave band set out.

Jamie's heart pounded. His feet skimmed the earth of the land that would be his home—and someday, God willing, his children and grandchildren would enjoy the same spirit of freedom that rang in the cold air. The group had marched about a mile by the seaside when the command came, "Halt!" Jamie froze and peered ahead. The bronzed forms of five or six men who must be Indians scattered, along with a barking dog.

"Come, we will see if we can find them and talk with them," Captain Standish ordered. "We must also discover if others are lying in ambush."

Jamie clutched his musket with sweaty hands. Could he actually fire at a living human being, even if attacked? *Please, Father*, he silently prayed. *Don't let it happen.* He hated killing and had secretly planned how he would offer to catch fish for food and avoid being sent on hunting trips to bring in meat.

The Indians darted into the woods. The Pilgrims followed. Then the savages raced back onto the packed

JAMIE CLUTCHED HIS MUSKET WITH SWEATY HANDS.

sand of the shore and their pursuers couldn't keep up with them. They did, however, follow their tracks, with Jamie hoping they would not catch them. Several miles later, with night coming on, the newcomers made camp and posted sentries. Yet Jamie found himself yawning and undisturbed by anything other than the usual night noises.

For several days, they tried to find the Indians or one of their villages. Each time a sharp noise sounded, Jamie swallowed hard. He knew he was no coward, but he had little liking for an expedition that might be set on at any moment. Not only did they fail to find Indians or signs of them—except for luckless William Bradford who became tangled in an Indian deer-trap made from a noose attached to a bent tree—they got lost in a thicket that tore at their clothing and armor. Jamie felt like howling with laughter but his tongue lay thick from lack of water. The water they finally found offered refreshment, and the company went on.

This time they had success. Jamie's eyes opened wide

THE NEWCOMERS MADE CAMP .

at the sight of where a cabin had been. A great kettle remained and buried in heaps of sand, the Pilgrims found Indian baskets filled with ears of corn!

The second expedition set out in the small, open boat brought from England to use in shallow waters. Thirty men crowded the shallop, and this time, they found more signs of the Indians, and brought back corn and beans from two cabins covered with matted roofs. Great rejoicing followed. The discovery meant they had seed to plant corn the next year.

"This land is so different from Holland or England," Jamie told Prue.

"I know." She couldn't keep back a small sigh. "I will be so glad when we can get off this ship and into houses."

He shook his dark head. "Poor Prue. If you were a boy or man you could go exploring with us." He quickly added, "I'm glad you're not, though. I like you the way you are."

Again she blushed. Past sixteen now, she felt more

"I LIKE YOU THE WAY YOU ARE."

woman than girl, but hung back from having to be grown up too soon.

Prudence's wish proved vain. For three months the Pilgrims lived on the *Mayflower*. Yet many things happened during that time. Frail Dorothy Bradford, William's wife, drowned. More expeditions led to the *Mayflower* leaving Provincetown and sailing for Plymouth Harbor, which was named after the English town from which they had set sail. Exploring bands encountered hostile Indians, but valiantly fought and drove them away. One of the groups was forced to seek refuge on an island in Plymouth Harbor during a blinding snowstorm. Just before Christmas, the men discovered a clear, running stream, a high hill suitable for setting up protection, and some cleared land. They later learned the site had once been an Indian village but a smallpox epidemic had swept through a few years earlier and wiped out the tribe.

Now the work doubled and tripled. A "common house" about twenty feet square came first. Then thatched huts

EXPLORING BANDS ENCOUNTERED HOSTILE INDIANS.

were built along the brook. Dugouts, caves dug into the hillsides, followed. Bark huts that looked much like Indian lodges were also constructed. Prudence and her family lived in a tiny cabin that had been hastily built. Although it offered protection from the winter, she couldn't help remembering the spotless Dutch homes while she attacked the dirt and snow tracked in. The Pilgrims had found a foot of snow on the ground when they reached Plymouth, located across Cape Cod Bay from Provincetown. Snug and warm, the family planned and dreamed of the spring and summer when planting would be done.

One night, Prue looked around her family circle. Mother sat knitting. Grandfather and Father stood near the open fireplace with its leaping flames that heated the one-room house. The tangy smell of rabbit stew and the good aroma of baking bread filled the air. Clothing hung on wooden pegs. Benches, table, and chair—all wood and made by the men of the family—offered little comfort compared with what the settlers had left behind.

PRUDENCE AND HER FAMILY LIVED IN A TINY CABIN.

Abigail and Charity whispered secrets in a corner. "It is good to be here," Prudence suddenly said.

Prue's words fell into the quiet room like stones into a smooth pool of water. Father looked at his eldest daughter. She saw pride in his eyes. "Yes, it is. You have spoken well." He hesitated, and she waited, sensing something coming. She followed his gaze from musket and powder horn above the mantel to the spinning wheel and butter churn nearby.

"Daughter, the colony has need of you."

"Of me, Father?" Bewildered, she wrinkled her freckled nose. What could he mean?

"If Mother can spare you, our little children need to be taught so they can read the Holy Word. Some of the men asked if you would be willing to teach their young ones."

"Why—" she faltered. "Do you think I am able?"

A sweet smile brightened his serious face. "I think you are able to do anything our Good Lord asks of you, and I cannot imagine a more important task."

"YOU HAVE SPOKEN WELL."

Never one to dally over deciding, Prudence bent to stir the kettle of stew hanging on the crane in the fireplace. She turned. "I will do it." A wide smile crossed her face. "I must study hard, or those I teach will know more than their teacher."

They talked more about Prue's new duty during the meal, eaten from wooden trenchers with pewter spoons. The stew and fresh bread, plus mugs of foamy milk, satisfied appetites made large by hard work. The little girls clapped their hands in delight when Mother brought out a special treat: a thick pudding made of sugar and milk boiled together and topped with a tiny spoonful of molasses.

Prue's mind spun. To think she would be a teacher! What would Jamie say?

She found out soon enough. He popped in for a short visit before the early bedtime the industrious workers held to in order to be up and at chores before daylight.

"I have news for you," she told him, blue eyes sparkling. "I am to teach the little ones."

"I MUST STUDY HARD."

A look she didn't understand crept into his dark eyes and she only caught part of his low answer, but she thought he said something about one day teaching their little ones. Her cheeks bloomed like roses, and she quickly looked down. Listening to such talk from a man to whom she was not betrothed* was not modest.

Life in the New World kept people so busy they had little time to get into trouble yet now and then a quarrel arose or a discontented person said aloud, "We should never have come to this harsh land. Better to have died in England under the King's rule than to starve in America." While most of the Pilgrims didn't agree, yet they admitted the truth in the man's complaint. Food had grown scarce and many of the little band could not adjust to a different way of eating than they were used to. Work never got done. Besides cooking and cleaning, the women and girls had to mend badly worn clothes to make them do until time permitted spinning thread and weaving cloth for more. They also did things the

*engaged

SHE ONLY CAUGHT PART OF HIS LOW ANSWER.

men had no time for such as making torches from the heart of pine logs to light their homes. When spring came, they would dip wicks into melted tallow and make candles and get out the big kettles for boiling lye and fat to make soap. They also carried water for cooking, bathing, and washing clothes.

Yet through all the hard work ran the determination for the children to learn. Every morning except for the Sabbath, after the hardest chores had been done, Prue gathered her pupils for an hour or two of hard study. Stubby, grubby fingers learned to form letters and stumbling tongues to read. Sometimes she made a game of learning by saying, "John, if you have three apples and James has two, how many do you have?"

She had to laugh when the oldest of her pupils turned down the corners of his mouth and said, "Just three, ma'am. James isn't one to give away what's his."

But sympathy flowed from her when the tall, always-hungry-looking boy added in a low voice, "I wish we had just one apple, even a dried one for Ma to make

"I WISH WE HAD JUST ONE APPLE."

pie." He licked his lips and looked sad.

"We will," she promised. "When spring comes, we'll plow and plant and search the woods for berries and fruit-bearing trees."

Yet her eyes stung, for James piped up, "Pa says if we kin hang on this winter, we kin do anything. Teacher, d'you think God will make spring come earlier if we ask Him?"

Prue blinked hard and hugged the anxious little boy with the worried face of an old man. Her heart echoed his words in a silent prayer. *God, if we can just hang on...*

GOD, IF WE CAN JUST HANG ON.

SHE FEARED THE QUICK TAP ON THE CABIN DOOR .

# 4
# *Bitter Winter*

January and February of 1621 brought disaster. Weakened by the long journey, hard work, and the lack of proper food, the Pilgrims grew ill. Sickness hung over Plymouth Plantation, as it had come to be known, like a flock of black crows shadowing a cornfield. Every family had at least one member sick, and in some families, each person lay ill, unable to help loved ones.

Now the nursing duties Prudence had begun learning on the *Mayflower* took all her waking hours. The little school she loved disbanded. Merry cries of children changed to feeble whispers pleading for water. Death claimed victim after victim, in spite of all Prudence could do. So far, her own family, Jamie and his father, and a few others had escaped but as day followed sad day, too many marked in passing by quick funerals, she feared the quick tap on the little cabin door that summoned her and Mother. All too often every effort proved too little. She lost count of the time she drew a sheet or rude blanket over a still form and turned toward home, fighting tears, and stumbling from weariness.

Prudence grew thin. Every freckle stood out on her tired-looking face. Jamie begged her to stop working so hard but all she said was, "Tell the sickness to stop. Only then can I rest."

One good thing about the sad times was the coming together of the people. Illness and death touched both Separatist and Londoner families. Those who could, gladly did their own chores, then volunteered to care for neighbors' needs by cutting and bringing wood, and meat, and generally helping all they could.

Captain Myles Standish and Elder William Brewster miraculously stayed well, although scurvy and other disease claimed half of the brave band. Now barely fifty remained, only a few of whom hadn't gotten sick. In Prue's home, she numbly cared for Mother and Father, bringing cold cloths for their burning faces, trying

"ONLY THEN CAN I REST."

to still their tossing bodies when they, too, fell ill.

"God, give me strength to go on," became her prayer. A hundred times she felt she must simply sink to the earthen floor and die from sheer fatigue. The day kind neighbors took Charity and Abigail away passed in a haze of unbelief.

A few days later Grandfather followed. Prue had no time to mourn her terrible loss, or the loss of Jamie's father. Father and Mother still needed her.

Too tired to pray, she huddled on a hard, wooden bench and put her head down on her folded arms resting on the table that had heard the family's laughter and eager plans for spring. If she thought of how her little sisters and Grandfather would not be with them, she knew she would sob until she couldn't stop. So she turned her mind toward the Lord, thanking Him that her parents were slightly better.

A minute or hours later, she couldn't tell which, she awoke to find strong arms around her. Her head no longer lay on her arms, but against a firm shoulder. She

SHE TURNED HER MIND TO THE LORD, THANKING HIM.

opened her eyes and looked into Jamie's dear face, gaunt from worry.

"Beloved, I am here."

His rock-like presence did what she hadn't permitted herself to do. The dam holding back all the tears she should have cried when settler after settler, and child after child, died broke with a mighty rush. She clutched his rough, coarsely woven coat and let the flood come.

Jamie didn't try to stop her, but wisely let her cry until the ocean of tears soaked them as the tossing waves had done on the journey from England. Prue hiccupped and her breath caught. He handed her a white square and she blew her nose. "Th-thank you."

He tipped her chin up with a strong finger. "Prue, when all this is over, will you wed me? I cannot keep from speaking. All these days and weeks, with the fever and Indians skulking about, I've longed to have the right to really take care of you. Will you have me?"

She looked up through tear-filled eyes. How thin and pale he had grown! Shadows hid in his dark gaze

"WILL YOU WED ME?"

and sadness, yet a steady light glowed as well. *God, if it weren't for Jamie, how could I go on?* Her comment from on board the *Mayflower* now became a prayer. A new flood threatened. Her voice dropped to a whisper. "With all my heart," she promised. "By then Father and Mother—" Quick remembering brought her out of his arms and across the room to where they lay, still and white. For a single heartbeat, she feared God had taken them. She leaned forward and laid a hand first on Mother's forehead, then on Father's. Her fear turned to thankfulness.

"Praise our Father," she whispered to Jamie. "The fever has broken! They are sleeping naturally."

His arms circled her waist. "I will fetch meat for broth," he told her. "They will have need of it to grow strong."

Like a fresh ocean breeze, the good news flew in the little settlement so starved for hope and staggering from the loss of loved ones. Several days passed and no more grew ill. Now the colonists learned more of what had

A STEADY LIGHT GLOWED.

happened among the crew on board the *Mayflower*, which lay anchored, waiting for good weather to sail back to England. When the calamity had first come, the crew had hurried most of the remaining passengers ashore so they wouldn't give the fever to the crew. Yet many of their officers and strongest men, including the bosun, gunner, three quarter-masters, and the cook had died—in all, almost half their number.

Unlike the Pilgrims, the snarling crew had turned on one another. Afraid of catching the terrible sickness, those who had remained healthy had refused to care for their ill. If they died, they died.

The few passengers still on board had showed mercy and pity. They'd cared for the weak and dying, even the bosun and some others who had cursed and scoffed at them. The proud young bosun had confessed, "I don't deserve it, after the way I treated you. I now see you show your love like Christians while we let our comrades lie and die like dogs."

The day came when Prudence on her rounds, followed

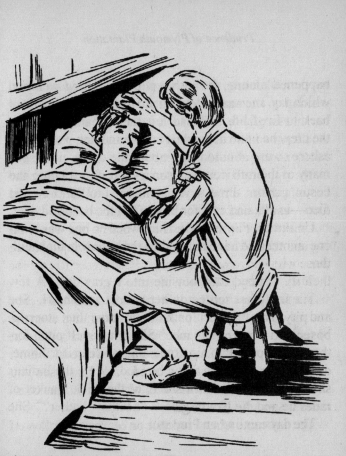

"I DON'T DESERVE IT, AFTER THE WAY I TREATED YOU."

by faithful Jamie, found her patients getting well and picking up life again, determined to go on in spite of the harshness of life that had left their small band even smaller and more dependent on one another. Father and Mother were able to creep about the cabin, nourished by the rich broth from venison a white-faced Jamie had brought them. Prue never mentioned to him how she knew what it had cost for him to kill the beautiful deer, but she put her arms around him when no one was looking and pressed her head against the hollow in his shoulder.

They stepped back outside into a gray day. A few lazy snowflakes settled on her bonnet and shawl. She started down the worn path to her home then stopped. "I feel so—Jamie, help me." She felt herself pitch forward, to be caught in his strong arms and carried. Somewhere in the distance a dog howled. Were the Indians coming? Why couldn't she fight the thick blanket of darkness reaching out for her? "Mother? Father?" She stopped struggling and lay still.

"JAMIE...HELP ME."

A long time later, Prudence opened her eyes. She lay on her own bed in the Simmons cabin. Her forehead wrinkled, and her throat felt dry. She turned her head. Jamie sat on the floor next to her, head bent as if in prayer. "Jamie?" It came out in a whispered croak.

The tousled dark head snapped up. "You're awake! Praise to our Father." He took her hand that lay on the coverlet. "Don't try to talk. You didn't have the fever. Elder Brewster said your body kept going as long as you needed to care for others, then it demanded a price for the long, hard days and weeks you've put in. Sleep, beloved. All is well."

Glad for his being there, she drifted back to sleep. The next time she awakened, Mother sat on a wooden chair next to her with a steaming mug in her hands. Spoonful by spoonful she fed Prue the way she would a baby until every drop disappeared.

Again Prue slept, and the third time she woke, she stretched and felt more like herself. Both Father and Mother sat near her. "God is good," Father said. His

"SLEEP BELOVED. ALL IS WELL."

work-worn hand stroked her hair. "He has spared one of our daughters." He cleared his throat and a faint sparkle crept into his eyes. "Although Master Lowe says if it be pleasing to Mother and myself, we may lose our eldest soon."

"You'll never lose me," Prue cried. "Jamie will fish and build me a home close by. If it pleases you," she quickly added.

"He's a fine lad, Prudence. He has proved that again and again." Father's face held new lines, but he smiled. "It 'minds me of how I felt when I met your mother."

Mrs. Simmons gazed at him. "You were also a fine lad and still are." She wiped a tear from the corner of her eye with her spotless apron. "One day there will be little ones." Prue knew she thought of Charity and Abigail, who waited in heaven for their coming, along with Grandfather, Mr. Lowe, and so many other dear friends. The next moment Mother stood. "Time to feed our patient again." This time she brought broth with

"ONE DAY THERE WILL BE LITTLE ONES."

vegetables and a piece of crusty bread. Nothing ever tasted better to Prue than the meal she always thought of as her betrothal meal.

In a few weeks, the hardworking nurse had gained back much of her health. Unable to do long tasks, she contented herself for a few days more in dreaming, taking walks when the March weather brought sunny days, and talking with Mother about the summer wedding she and Jamie planned. The ladies of the colony took time from their busy lives and gathered for a quilting bee from the patchwork cover and lining Mother had been saving. An even layer of wool went between and small, tight stitches fastened the quilt securely. Two little girls sat in a corner sewing strips of rags together for rugs. Prue blinked hard, wishing her sisters could be with them. Yet when she looked around the big quilt frame set like a table top over the back of four chairs, she silently gave thanks. One or two of the women had lost all their family. She still had Father, Mother, and Jamie.

THE HARD WORKING NURSE GAINED BACK HER HEALTH.

One day, she would have her family back again, because God had sent His Son to save all who believed on Him. Until then, those who followed Him had much to do in telling others of His love.

THOSE WHO FOLLOWED *HIM* HAD MUCH TO DO.

HIS NAME WAS SAMOSET.

# 5
## *Indians!*

Except for the scouting party skirmish and a few sightings of Indians, there had been no further real trouble. Still, the colonists remained prepared and built a fort on the hill. By the end of their second year, they planned to have a tall fence enclosing the houses and the fort, which was used as a church.

One day in mid-March, a lone Indian came to the settlement. Everyone ran from their homes to see the man who boldly walked in and began speaking in broken English. Prue and Jamie marveled. The Indian said his name was *Samoset*, and he was not of these parts but came from farther East. He was acquainted with English ships that came to fish. He named them and proudly added that was where he got his language.

The colonists learned many important things about Samoset's people for he was a chief of the Pemaquid tribe. He also told them of another Indian, a native named *Squanto*, who had been in England. Samoset came again and brought others, who returned tools stolen by some of them while the colonists had left their work to eat dinner.

"Squanto sounds like someone who can really help us," the leaders rejoiced. Yet no one realized just how much the Patuxet Indian would mean to their survival.

The entire settlement gasped when the native folded his arms and told his exciting, but sad, story. Born sometime about 1585, Squanto, also called *Tisquantum*, showed little emotion except in his glittering black eyes while he spoke.

"In 1614, English fishermen took me away from my country and my people," he began. "I was taken to Spain and sold as a slave. Pah! No Patuxet shall be slave to a white man. I stayed long years but my heart called me to come home. First, I lived in Newfoundland." He glanced into the surrounding forests. "By the time I came back here, most of my tribe had died. Only a few

"I WAS SOLD AS A SLAVE."

lived and they had joined the Wampanoag, whose chief is the mighty warrior, Massasoit."

Governor Carver spoke quietly. "Squanto, will you help us? You lost most of your people. So have we. More than half have died of sickness and starvation since we came a few months ago. Our food is almost gone. We want no trouble with your people."

Squanto fixed his dark gaze on the governor, "Massasoit and the Wampanaog are angry. Your people stole their corn."

"Yes, we did, and it was wrong."

The frank admission seemed to convince Squanto. "I will talk with Massasoit, and if he will come, I will bring him to you so there will be peace between my tribe and yours." He turned and marched away.

Prue told Jamie, "If white people had stolen me and treated me as Squanto has been treated, I don't think I would be so willing to help them."

"He is a great man," Jamie replied. His eyes showed how much he admired their visitor.

"HE IS A GREAT MAN."

Squanto had been bold and friendly, but Massasoit strode into the settlement as if he owned it. He appeared to be perhaps five or so years older than Squanto and stood as tall and straight as one of his own arrows. Prudence though he looked more kingly in his scanty clothing that made her gaze only on his face (so she wouldn't blush!) than King James ever had in all his silks, satins, and ruffs. He greeted Governor Carver with all the dignity of royalty and surrounded by his chief friends, sat without moving through the refreshments and the gifts the colonists had brought for this very purpose.

At last came time to talk terms for lasting peace. Massasoit, through Squanto, who interpreted, agreed that as long as he lived he and his tribe would obey the treaty if the white people did the same.*

"Neither he nor any of his people, shall injure or do hurt to any of your people," Squanto said. "If any of them do hurt, Massasoit will send that person so you

*Massasoit kept the peace all of his life and died in 1661, which was a very old age for a man of his times—about 80.

HE AND HIS TRIBE WOULD OBEY THE TREATY.

can punish him.

"If anything is taken away from any of your people, he will see that it is brought back and you must do the same.

"If any justly war against him you will aid him. If any war against you, he and his tribe will aid you.

"Massasoit will tell his neighboring tribes of the agreement that they might not wrong the settlers but likewise consent to the conditions of peace.

"When Massasoit and his people come to the settlement, they will leave their bows and arrows behind them."

Squanto's deep voice ceased. Prue, from a good listening place that did not intrude on the talk, felt her heart lift. Surely, God had sent Squanto to them, the same way He'd sent Moses to be a deliverer to his people and a protector in the wilderness!

The talks ended and peace began. Massasoit and his braves left for Sowams, some forty miles from Plymouth,

PRUE FELT HER HEART LIFT.

but Squanto listened to the pleadings of the settlers.

"Stay with us, Squanto," they told him. "Teach us the things you know that we do not, so our people may live."

A faint flicker in the dark eyes made Prue wonder if Squanto felt surprise that white men, who usually treated Indians like they were little better than beasts of the forest, should ask such a thing. The corners of his mouth lifted just a little bit. "I will stay," he said.

At the next meeting, the settlers gave thanks to God for sending such help. Squanto knew everything about his own country. He showed them how to raise the finest corn, beans and pumpkins by planting dead herring with the seeds. He showed them the best places to fish and hunt. One day, William Bradford would write about his gratefulness and about how Squanto took the men to various places and showed them ways to survive in the New World.

Just when life appeared to be settling down, another sad event took place. John Carver, the beloved governor,

"I WILL STAY."

died less than a month after making the treaty with Massasoit. One hot April day, he complained of a terrible head pain, lay down, and died within a few days. The diminished group mourned and buried him in the best manner they could, with volleys of shot by all who bore arms.

Choosing a new governor meant serious consideration, and William Bradford, now thirty-two, was selected. One of the first things Bradford did was to send a mission to Massasoit and make sure that friendly relations and the treaty would be strengthened. Squanto stayed with the Pilgrims and showed them how to gather clams and catch eels for food.

Spring had never been more welcome. Prudence sang at her tasks, and they felt lighter now that winter had gone, and her wedding day drew closer. Jamie and the other colonists were equally busy. It took all kinds of workers to keep the settlement going. That first spring required long hours and many hands to clear and till land. In their spare time at home, farmers had to make

"I WILL STAY."

died less than a month after making the treaty with Massasoit. One hot April day, he complained of a terrible head pain, lay down, and died within a few days. The diminished group mourned and buried him in the best manner they could, with volleys of shot by all who bore arms.

Choosing a new governor meant serious consideration, and William Bradford, now thirty-two, was selected. One of the first things Bradford did was to send a mission to Massasoit and make sure that friendly relations and the treaty would be strengthened. Squanto stayed with the Pilgrims and showed them how to gather clams and catch eels for food.

Spring had never been more welcome. Prudence sang at her tasks, and they felt lighter now that winter had gone, and her wedding day drew closer. Jamie and the other colonists were equally busy. It took all kinds of workers to keep the settlement going. That first spring required long hours and many hands to clear and till land. In their spare time at home, farmers had to make

PRUDENCE SANG AT HER TASKS.

shoes, furniture, and other necessary articles.

Jamie, of course, set to fishing, and rejoiced at the harbors and abundance of fish. He caught more than needed, so he cleaned and dried them so they wouldn't spoil. He could make a good living by shipping them to markets in Europe in exchange for cloth and goods.

Whale hunting provided blubber* that was boiled into whale oil. Many settlers used it in crude lamps to light their homes.

The sailors, fishermen, and whalers needed sturdy ships, so some of the colonists worked at cutting trees and building ships, then cut and stitched heavy canvas to make the large while sails.

Prudence never tired of watching the coopers who made the wooden storage barrels used to keep—and later ship—fish, rum, molasses, and whale oil. A few colonial families who were better off, hired cabinetmakers to build beautiful tables, chairs, and even wooden panels to cover rough walls.

---

*whale fat

SOME OF THE COLONISTS WORKED AT BUILDING SHIPS.

Jamie preferred visiting with the blacksmith, as did the children. The smoky shop had pieces of glowing iron which became horseshoes, tools, and nails.

One morning, Mr. Simmons awakened with a swollen jaw and aching tooth. When the pain refused to stop, he reluctantly made his way to the blacksmith shop. The smith took iron pincers, fastened them on the aching tooth, and with a mighty wrench yanked it out. Father came home sweating and holding his jaw.

"How could you bear it?" tender-hearted Prue cried.

"Daughter, the moments of pain were awful, but so was having the tooth just ache and ache," Father mumbled.

Even the Sabbath meetings were more enjoyable now that spring had come. No longer must families bundle into every warm article of clothing they possessed to keep from freezing in the unheated meetinghouse. Even the foot warmers, those little metal boxes filled with hot coals from fireplaces, helped only during the first part of the long sermons. The heat from the coals died

"THE MOMENTS OF PAIN WERE AWFUL."

long before the meeting ended.

Prue sometimes wanted to smile at the tithingman who walked up and down carrying a long rod. If anyone dozed or nodded, he tickled them with the feathers on one end of the rod but if someone fell asleep, the tithingman gave him or her a whack on the head with the knob on the other end. Prudence took care to sit up straight on the hard wooden pew and concentrate on the elder who stood in a high pulpit. She found it hard when the sermon sometimes lasted five hours.

"Father," she prayed one Sabbath evening before she went to bed. "I don't mean to be disrespectful, but the sermons are so long, and the days so sunny and inviting! My mind wanders like the butterfly that flew in through the open window." She yawned and fell asleep.

❖

Little by little, the people settled into their lives in the New World. Squanto's advice about planting proved to be good. Fields of growing corn, beans, and pumpkins stood strong in the cleared patches of the forest. gover-

"MY MIND WANDERS ..."

nor Bradford and the other leaders led the people in praise and thankfulness. When winter came once more, food aplenty would be prepared for the cold months.

FOOD APLENTY WOULD BE PREPARED.

PRUDENCE AND JAMIE WERE MARRIED.

# 6
## *A New Adventure*

Prudence and Jamie were married in a simple ceremony and without fuss. However, the colonists banded together to get the young couple started. They gave from their own limited stores and Prudence loved her cozy, new cabin—raised by the men of the settlement. Jamie worked hard fishing, and as summer passed, curtains brightened their glassless window. When winter came, they would close the heavy wooden shutter Jamie had made and one day, they'd have a real glass.

Although most of the Indians remained friendly and peaceful, not all liked the English. The people of Plymouth Plantation were horrified when an Indian named Hobomok, who had come to live with the settlers, returned from a journey into the forest with terrible news. Jamie burst through the little cabin's open door. "I fear Squanto has been killed," he told her. "A hostile sachem* called Corbitant started a quarrel with Hobomok and Squanto about fourteen miles west of here. Corbitant said he was going to stab our friends." He stopped for breath, his dark eyes flashing.

"But why?" Prue cried. Every freckle stood out clear on her nose and cheeks. Dread filled her heart.

"Just because they are friendly and serve us," Jamie said. "Hobomok got away but he's afraid that Squanto's dead." He reached for his musket that always hung over the mantel. His face paled. His lips set. "Pray there will be no bloodshed over this. Governor Bradford says if we don't stop this now, no Indians will ever be friendly again. Corbitant and others like him will kill those who are, then start to massacre us."

"Oh, Jamie, be careful." Prue bit her lip to keep from begging him to stay. Their governor was right. The men must protect those of the settlement, red or white.

Jamie marched away with the memory of her upturned face and blue eyes that reflected both fear and her faith

---

*chief

116

"PRAY THERE WILL BE NO BLOODSHED OVER THIS."

in him. With every step into the forest, he prayed mightily. Hobomok guided the company of the Captain and fourteen men on the night rescue raid on the fourteenth of August. They reached the house where Corbitant was thought to be. Jamie's heart thumped until it seemed the whole countryside would hear and be warned. He prayed some more.

"Thank God!" many exclaimed when the rescuers learned that Squanto had only been threatened, not stabbed. The other Indians there knew nothing of Corbitant's wicked doings and brought forth provisions. Three who had been hurt by breaking out of the house and attempting to get through the guard, were taken back to the settlement, their wounds dressed, then sent back to their homes. This brought good will from the Indians and more peace. Even Corbitant stopped his persecutions, although he refused to come near the settlement for a long, long time.

❖

Fall passed in a frenzy of preserving and drying and

HOBOMOK GUIDED THE COMPANY.

making houses snug against the coming winter. In November, the small ship *Fortune* arrived with thirty-five passengers who needed shelter, as they were to remain and work on Plymouth Plantation. The colonists arranged for a cargo of beaver skins and clapboards to go back on the ship's return voyage. However, a far more important matter had to be settled before the *Fortune* sailed.

Prue and Jamie discussed what was happening. Before the Pilgrims had left England, they had refused to sign the unsatisfactory contract Robert Cushman, their agent, had drawn up. Now here he was among them to get the necessary signatures.

"His sermon in the common house wasn't a sermon at all," Prue disgustedly said. "All he wanted to do was to get our leaders to sign and close his old contract."

"He succeeded, didn't he?" Jamie grinned. His face turned serious. "It's good to have more people, but they have come so ill-prepared! No food, no bedding, no pots, no pans. They're young and strong, but we who

"HE SUCCEEDED, DIDN'T HE?"

have been here will have to take care of them."

"At least we can give thanks for the abundance of food," Prudence reminded. "This time last year we were in a sad condition."

"I know." Jamie recovered his high spirits. Like a boy, he clasped his hands in anticipation. "Governor Bradford says we are to have a celebration soon, a time of giving thanks for our blessings. It is to last three days, and Massasoit and his tribe will be honored guests."

Soon, Jamie, Prue, and every member of the settlement were involved in preparing for the three-day thanksgiving celebration. The Indians acted pleased with their invitation and responded by bringing gifts of venison and wild turkeys. The men brought wild ducks and geese. Jamie and a few friends fished even longer hours than usual. Shellfish and eels added to the feast.

Children gathered nuts and watercress; they also took turns turning the great spits on which the meat cooked over open fires. Prue made so much succotash of corn

"WE ARE TO HAVE A CELEBRATION SOON."

and beans she secretly wondered if she could ever enjoy eating it again. Corn meal bread, journey cake, and every other kind of baked goods the women could manage, filled the air with their aromas. Enormous plank tables stood outdoors. Even the common house used for meetings could never hold all those joyous persons who came together in peace and gratitude toward their Heavenly Father.

Prue never felt strange around Squanto, but Massasoit's tall figure made her a little uneasy. Sometimes she wondered if the chief, who appeared to take his duties so seriously, ever laughed. The same was not true of many of his tribe. They chattered away in their own language, grunted, poked one another in the ribs— and oh, how they could eat!

"Will there be any left for us?" A small boy clutched Prue's long apron and peered out from behind her.

Her hand rested on his rough hair. "There is so much food none will go hungry," she promised. He heaved a sigh of relief and became bold enough to step out and

"WILL THERE BE ANY LEFT FOR US?"

toward the tables crowded with good food, but when an Indian glanced his way, he scuttled back behind his protector.

"If only all the Indians could be our friends," Prue sighed to Jamie when their visitors had finally gone and all traces of the long feast were taken away. She thought of the snakeskin tied to a bundle of arrows that the great tribe of Narragansetts had recently sent. Interpreters said this was a threat and a challenge. Governor Bradford and his counselors didn't back down. They sent word that the colonists had done the Indians no wrong, but if the Narragansetts would rather have war than peace, to come when they would. The message also said that the Pilgrims weren't afraid, and that the Indians should come knowing they'd find the settlers armed and ready to fight. They returned the arrow-filled snakeskin, but it came back again. However, no attack followed.

"Our homes are enclosed with a strong fence, and guards keep watch in the night," Jamie comforted. "If any cry of fire or danger comes, all the men are ready to

GOVENOR BRADFORD DIDN'T BACK DOWN.

fight."

A funny happening on Christmas Day made Prudence smile. As usual, the governor called the men out to work. Most of the newcomers, who should have been grateful for the way the earlier Pilgrims opened their homes and shared, refused to work, saying it was against their consciences.

Governor Bradford excused them, only to later discover the men playing in the streets at stool-ball.* He immediately told them it was against *his* conscience for them to play while others worked, and made them stop. "If you are to keep this day as a matter of devotion," he said, "Keep it in your houses. There will be no gaming or reveling in the streets."

❖

The second winter passed far easier than the first. Yet spring brought more threats of Indian trouble, and rumors of attacks kept the settlers on guard. Hobomok thought them false, as they proved to be. Governor

---

*a game where balls were driven from stool to stool

"ALL THE MEN ARE READY TO FIGHT."

Bradford found to his dismay that Squanto appeared to be changing. If gossip were to be believed, their faithful servant hadn't been able to resist using his position of trust with the English to his own advantage. Stories ran on the wind that Squanto had made the Indians believe he could stir up war or make peace when he chose, and that he could call a plague from the ground if he wanted to. The Indians willingly gave him gifts and began to depend more on Squanto than on Massasoit.

When Massasoit learned of this, Squanto's life was in danger for wanting to take his leader's place with the tribe. He fled back to the English and stayed close to the settlement until he died of a fever later in 1622. The people genuinely missed him. Whatever else he was, Squanto had been a true friend in a time of the Pilgrims' great need.*

❖

By late spring, provisions were again low. The colo-

---

*Records show that Squanto accepted the Lord before he died, saying he wanted to go to "the Englishmen's God in heaven."

SQUANTO'S LIFE WAS IN DANGER.

nists waited in vain for trading ships. In May, a shallop arrived with seven passengers and letters, but no food, in spite of many promises. The elders in meeting quoted verses that reminded the people to trust in God, not in other folks' promises.

Reports from other small groups brought the fear of trouble. Some in want had stolen the Indians' corn and had angered them. Would their thievery put Plymouth Plantation in danger? "I guess hungry people will do all kinds of things," Jamie said one night while Prue knitted a soft garment. Soon a little Prudence or Jamie would come to their home in the New World that was now their own world.

"I know." Her fingers stilled from her work and a sad look crept into her face. "Father said today some of Mr. Weston's men are in such great want, they have done terrible things! When the Indians would not lend corn to John Sanders, left in charge at the Bay of Massachusetts, he wrote and asked our governor for permission to take the corn by force." She scowled. "When Gover-

A SAD LOOK CREPT INTO HER FACE.

nor Bradford said no, Sanders' men went and told the Indians our governor planned to come take the corn."

"They are selling clothes and bed clothing," Jamie put in. "A few have become servants to the Indians."

Prudence gasped. "Truly?"

"Truly. They cut wood and fetch water for a cap full of corn. Others steal what they can get away with. Some have starved—and all because they wasted their plentiful supply instead of using it wisely."

Prue looked around her snug home, feeling sorry for the unfortunate persons and wishing they had managed better.

"At least we have good news about Massasoit," Jamie said. He leaned back in his hard chair and smiled. "Massasoit isn't going to die after all. The medicine and comfort we sent healed him. He's going among the tribes trying to undo the harm done by Weston's men." A dark look crossed his face. "I fear what will happen if he isn't believed."

A DARK LOOK CROSSED HIS FACE.

THEY FOUND WAYS TO HAVE FUN.

# 7
## *Fun and Fear*

Not all of life in Plymouth Colony was grim. Although the need to make a home in the New World and be alert to possible dangers remained constantly before the Pilgrims, in their spare time and sometimes even in their work, they found ways to have fun. House and barn raisings, where the men and older boys worked building while the women and girls cooked and baked and served enormous meals, brought a time to visit with one another. So did the quilting bees.

In late summer and fall when geese were killed, women separated the large and small feathers. The small ones became stuffing for feather beds. The large quills were set aside until winter offered time enough to have a "feather-stripping" party. Many families crowded into a warm kitchen. Babies slept on wide, feather beds. Prudence and Jamie loved the good smell of popping popcorn and boiling syrup for taffy. First, the soft down must be stripped from thousands of feathers to provide filling for cushions and quilts. Laughter made the messy job seem not so hard, yet sometimes Prue secretly envied the children old enough not to be put to bed but too young to feather-strip. Their cries of joy rang from the happiness of skating on the solid ice formed by snapping cold winter nights.

As happened so many times, Jamie seemed able to read her thoughts. "We'll skate again," he whispered. "After our baby comes."

Prue smiled and felt thankful that of all the prettier girls and young women, Jamie had chosen her.

"Suppertime!" their host called. A little murmur of anticipation swept through the workers. Roast goose, cold venison, hot biscuits or corn bread, gingerbread, and sweet cider tasted good after the feather-stripping. So did the popcorn and taffy. Tucked into a sleigh when the merry evening ended, Prue couldn't help thinking again how different things were from the first year, when

"WE WILL SKATE AGAIN... AFTER OUR BABY COMES."

so many people sickened and died.

Another fall get-together came when the corn needed to be husked and shelled. A corn husking bee drew large groups of helpers, who worked hard and husked hundreds of ears of corn, then shelled it into bushels.

❖

In late winter, Jamie, Mr. Simmons, and the other men and boys went into the woods to see if clear liquid on the twig ends meant the sap had begun to run in the sugar maple trees. When this happened, they bored holes into the tree trunks and put in spouts and hung wooden buckets so the sap could drip into them. The sap then was allowed to boil into maple syrup. Some of it boiled much longer and became maple sugar. The only thing Jamie didn't like this year was having to stay at the sugar camp for a few days until the job ended. Soon his and Prue's baby would arrive. Yet, he knew she loved the maple candy made by pouring hot syrup on clean snow and allowing it to cool, and he came home carrying maple sugar and maple syrup and telling her with his

SAP HAD BEGUN TO RUN IN THE SUGARMAPLE TREES.

smile how good it was to be with her.

Baby James was born just a few days after the sugaring off. Now Prue understood the look she had seen on other women's faces. Jamie was so proud of his son, he came very close to being guilty of the sin of boasting! Little James had a pair of lungs guaranteed to get attention and his young parents rejoiced in his good health. For a time, they let worry about the Indian troubles slip from their minds.

Others did not. Mr. Weston had heard of the ruin in his colony. Angry and saddened, he disguised himself as a blacksmith and went to find out about it. He had little skill in battling a storm, and his shallop went to the bottom of the bay! He barely escaped with his life. To make things worse, he fell into the hands of a tribe of Indians who took what little he had saved and all his clothes except his shirt. Days later he got to a village, borrowed a suit of clothing, and came to Plymouth to borrow beaver skins. He promised that when a ship came to him, he'd give them supplies.

JAMIE WAS SO PROUD OF HIS SON.

After consideration, he was given one hundred beaver skins. Later Jamie disgustedly told Prue, "Ungrateful wretch! He never repaid anything and goes about saying harsh things. I have a feeling he will be our enemy." It proved true.

Until now, the people had all worked for the common good. Governor Bradford talked with his counselors and started a new plan. Each family was assigned a parcel of land for their own present use (but not as an inheritance to be passed down to their children and grandchildren). This way, the families could trust themselves for raising the crops they needed. A lot of trouble had come from trying to have everyone work for each other. Women resented having to wash other men's clothes. Young men felt it wrong to be working to support others instead of their own wives and children. The older men felt they weren't being respected.

While Baby James grew, many other things took place that affected the colonists. Greedy persons tried to sue and get their hands on other people's properties. Ships

" I HAVE A FEELING HE WILL BE OUR ENEMY. "

set sail and battered themselves against jagged rocks.

A new danger loomed. Terrible drought came. No rain fell from the third week of May until mid-July. No more did laughter sound, except among the very young children. The corn withered and died, and if it had not been planted with dead fish, as Squanto had taught the settlers, it would have had no moisture at all. Yet, the dryer grounds were parched like withered hay and were useless and hopeless.

In great distress, the leaders called for part of a day to be set apart in what they called "a solemn day of humiliation."

"We will seek the Lord," Mrs. Simmons told Prue, eyes filled with hope. In humble and continued prayer, the people prayed. For all of the morning and the greater part of the day, the skies stayed clear and boiling hot. Not one cloud broke their blueness. As evening neared, however, the skies turned gray and rained gentle, earth-healing showers. There was no wind. There was no thunder, as often came with the rain. Just a soaking rain

"WE WILL SEEK THE LORD."

that healed the parched earth.

To the settlers' joy and the Indians' amazement, the corn and other crops revived and provided a large harvest, for the rain continued to fall like God's blessings mixed in with a fair, warm weather.

A few weeks later about 60 new persons, some of them wives and children of the earlier Pilgrims, arrived and took their place in the colony. Some trembled at the poor conditions they found and wanted to return to England. Others felt sad for the hardship they knew their friends had withstood. Governor Bradford wrote in his journal the words Prudence and Jamie clung to, "God gives health and strength in good measure." The young man's fishing provided much of the food from the sea.

The governor also wisely settled trouble about food before it started. He ordered the newcomers to keep and use the food they had brought while the settlers had to stick with what they had raised until the harvest, unless they bought by purchase or exchange. Both sides

"GOD GIVES HEALTH AND STRENGTH IN GOOD MEASURE."

went away satisfied. The new people were as much afraid the hungry planters would consume their provisions as the colonists were that by sharing their few stores, they would go hungry.

As soon as the harvest came, famine ended for a time, at least, and the people rejoiced. Some of the planters, including the Simmons family and Jamie and Prue, had raised enough extra to be able to sell some of their food, and no one wanted for anything.

With the coming in of new families, some of who had grand ideas about getting rich and building fancy houses, an agreement had to be made. Governor Bradford drew up some simple rules:

1. He and the Pilgrims would welcome and offer love and friendship to the strangers and give them places to live in the town.

2. The new people must obey all laws and orders of the colony.

3. Other than helping defend the colony, etc.,

GOVENOR BRADFORD DREW UP SOME SIMPLE RULES.

those who were not of the body of Pilgrims but had come on their own and for themselves would be free from general employment of the community.

4. Every male sixteen and older must pay a bushel of Indian wheat toward the maintenance of the governor and public officers.

5. According to the agreement with merchants, made before they had come, the ones working for themselves and not the good of the community could not trade with the Indians for furs or other items.

About this time a Captain Gorges arrived and so did Mr. Weston. Captain Gorges had been appointed to be general Governor of the country. He immediately charged Weston with causing much trouble with the Indians by what his men had done, along with some other charges. Weston said he had no responsibility. His men had done things on their own. He grew angry and threw

CAPTAIN GORGES ARRIVED.

such a fit that Captain Gorges threatened to send him back to England.

Letters sailed back and forth, often with false news about the colony. All kinds of wild accusations were made and quarrels arose. Some wicked men brought shame on the settlement with their actions. Trials followed, and the guilty were put out of the church.

"I sometimes long for the earlier years." Prue sighed one evening and nestled close the tiny daughter who bore her name. "Even though times were hard, we didn't have all the wickedness that is now taking place."

"I know, and it is going to lead to terrible war between the Indians and the innocent, as well as those who are giving the tribes muskets. They are also misbehaving with the Indian women, and a man named Morton has taught the braves how to load and fire and hunt game with the guns instead of with bows and arrows. Now, the Indians have their own moulds to make bullets and they are better fitted out than we are," Jamie added. He shook his curly dark head and his eyes looked sad.

"IT IS GOING TO LEAD TO TERRIBLE WAR."

"When war comes, and it cannot help but come in spite of all Massasoit does to keep it back, lead will be scarce, yet the Indians will have it. Even now, we're hearing of incidents in other villages where friends and neighbors are being killed by Indians." He stopped and stared at her. "Prue, shall we return to England?"

She started to shake her head violently, then stopped. Would living in England be any better than here with the threat of attack? She looked at her children, then at Jamie. "No. We knew when we came there would be danger. All we can do now is to trust God to protect us and pray that war will not come."

"ALL WE CAN DO NOW IS TRUST GOD TO PROTECT US."

"HE'S GOT TO BE STOPPED."

# 8
## *Danger for Jamie*

"He's got to be stopped." White-faced but stern, Jamie Lowe stood among his fellow men, strong arms crossed. Still young in years, he had proved himself worthy of respect, and when he spoke, others listened. "There's no other way," he went on. "Twice we have sent messages warning Thomas Morton that his sins are not just his own. He is putting everyone in danger through his wickedness."

"Aye," cried the leaders of the other plantations with whom the Plymouth men had met. Although Plymouth Plantation had the least fear of Indian uprising because of Massasoit's treaty and his influence on other tribes, they recognized the danger signals that could spread to their people as well.

Jamie had spoken truly. When Morton continued to stir up the Indians, the group of leaders first wrote to him in a friendly way, asking that he stop his trouble-some doings.

Morton laughed in the messengers' faces, then sneered. "Who are you to tell me what to do?" he de-manded. "I have and will trade guns with the Indians. I will also do as I please in my personal life, and it's none of your business. Tell those old busybodies who sent you to keep their long noses for sniffing and not poke them into others' affairs."

A second message met an even worse reception. He ignored the facts presented by the Pilgrims, which were, "You, Thomas Morton, are injuring this country. Be advised it is against our common safety and against the king's orders."

Morton replied, "The king's order is worthless. Tell me, what is the penalty? Who cares if the king is dis-pleased? Besides, the king is dead and his displeasure died with him." He scowled and added, "If anyone thinks he can come and tell me what to do, that man had better think again. I will be prepared." He held out one hand

"WHO ARE YOU TO TELL ME WHAT TO DO ?!"

and clenched it into a fist.

Now the gathered men appealed to Governor Bradford. "Will you send Captain Standish and aides to arrest Morton? If he continues on the path he's chosen, woe be to us all!"

"Captain Standish?" Governor Bradford looked at the short man standing nearby. "Will you go?"

"I will." Standish stepped forward.

"Who will you have to go with you?"

Jamie held his breath but didn't flinch when the captain pointed to him and said, "I'll have young Lowe, there. He's a strapping man." Standish also chose others.

An hour later, the little band set out. Prudence watched from the door of hers and Jamie's little home. James jumped up and down chanting, "Father's going hunting," for Jamie carried his musket over his shoulder. Little Prue waved her baby hand.

"Be careful," Prudence whispered.

"I will." Yet Jamie couldn't summon a smile. Even

"I WILL."

now that he was older, the idea of killing filled him with dread. How would Morton meet the unwelcome visitors, come to take him back to be tried for his sins? *Not without a fight,* Jamie decided. The prayer, *Please, God, don't let there be killing* kept time with his steady steps while he followed Captain Standish.

Morton had carried out his threat. When his enemies arrived, the outlaw had his doors shut and made fast. His men stood armed and waiting. Dishes of powder and bullets sat ready on the table. But he had made one terrible mistake. He and his friends had also armed themselves with false courage by drinking heavily.

"Thomas Morton, come out." Captain Standish's voice sounded loud, even through the walls and shut doors.

He answered by cursing and shouting, but a little later, fearing the attackers would harm the house, he and part of his crew did come out—not to surrender, but to shoot.

Jamie saw them come. His sweaty hand clutched his musket. Then his lips twitched. His sense of humor

"THOMAS MORTON, COME OUT!"

made him want to laugh.  Morton and his men were so drunk they could barely lift their heavy guns!  Morton had a carbine, later found to be over-charged, almost half full of powder and shot.  He aimed it at Captain Standish, but Standish leaped forward, grabbed the gun, and took Morton.  In the confusion that followed, Jamie feared the worst.  It didn't happen.  The only person hurt in the entire capture was one of Morton's men.  He was so drunk, he ran his nose into the point of a sword and lost a little of his hot blood!

The next ship for England carried both Morton and letters to the authorities concerning the man, enough to prosecute him. To the settlers' disgust, nothing was done to him. He wasn't even reprimanded, and the next year, he returned to America, where before long, he started his old tricks. This time when he was arrested and again sent to England, Morton ended up in Exeter Gaol on a suspected murder charge.  His house in New England was destroyed so others couldn't gather there to plot.

Again, he got free and wrote a book that Governor

STANDISH GRABBED THE GUN AND TOOK MORTON.

Bradford called, "Full of lies and slander and profanity." Years later, Morton returned to America when wars raged in England. He was thrown into prison in Boston for the book and other wicked things, released after a year, and given a heavy fine. Morton died in Maine, with no record that he had ever repented of his terrible sins.

In the meantime, Jamie and his fellow settlers could relax a bit, free of the evil influence Morton had spread.

Other persons proved treacherous in their dealings, as well. Sometimes shippers didn't keep their word and cheated the colonists about goods coming into and out of the country. More and more people came to America, some well prepared, but most with little to their name. The Dutch as well as the English saw in America the chance to own land and to be their own masters, perhaps even to grow rich.

So good and bad, rich and poor, hard-working and lazy mingled. Laws had to be enforced, but tenderhearted Prudence could hardly bear some of the cruel

JAMIE AND HIS FELLOW SETTLERS COULD RELAX.

punishments given to those who sinned. Some lost their right to vote and have a say in the rules by which they must live. Time after time, Prue looked down at her feet to keep from seeing friends and neighbors locked in the stocks—boards that had holes through which their feet were placed. Anyone caught telling a lie must sit there for hours, and the whole village pointed and laughed.

Even worse, the pillory, which was a platform with boards with holes for head and hands to go through, meant long, hard hours of misery and shame.

Prudence and Jamie never went near to the public whippings given to those who sinned. But they felt one of the worst punishments was the ducking stool.

"I don't care if Mrs. Doan does gossip and nag her husband," Prue cried, tears of anger in her eyes. "The men who tie her in a chair at the end of that wooden pole over the pond and take joy in ducking her up and down in the cold water are worse than a gossip or nag!"

"Shhh, don't say that too loudly," Jamie warned.

THE PILLORY.

"Laws are strict." He looked doubtful. "I don't like it, either. Jesus told us to forgive as He did. I can't imagine Him treating people this way. Perhaps one day, we will learn to be more like Him."

Prudence dried her wet eyes, but her heart still ached. "What would you do if they came for me and put me on the ducking stool?"

His lips set in a straight line. His eyes darkened. "I promised you long ago in Holland I would always take care of you, didn't I? I'd like to see anyone try to harm or shame you in any way."

Comforted by the love and understanding of her tall, strong husband, Prudence again thanked God for him.

❖

The years passed in hard work and fun. James and little Prudence grew, filled with questions. They never tired of hearing how their parents and grandparents had come to the New World or of hearing stories about the *Mayflower*. James proved a true son of his father. From the time he could toddle, he enjoyed going out in the fish-

"WE WILL LEARN TO BE MORE LIKE HIM."

ing boat with his father and each year, his hands grew more sturdy and capable until he became a good helper.

Likewise, Prudence was her mother's joy. She learned to spin and weave, bake and sew. Whatever Prue did, her daughter longed to try. One of her favorite tasks was to help make candles. When her mother said, "Tomorrow is candle-dipping day," Prudence clapped her hands. The next morning, she stood back while Prue hung a great iron pot on the crane in the fireplace and put in all the beef and sheep fat she had saved. Prudence learned to sit near the fireplace and slowly keep the kettle swinging over the hot coals.

Soon, the hot fat melted into tallow. Now, Prue set two chairs back to back and a ways apart, then laid two poles across them. Young Prudence helped her mother cut strings called wicks that were twice as long as the candles would be, twist them double, and tie them on slender rods a few inches apart.

Prudence always held her breath when her mother carefully lifted the great pot of melted tallow from the

YOUNG PRUDENCE HELPED HER MOTHER.

fire to the floor. Then came the fun part, one Prudence learned to do well. She held out a rod and lowered it until the wicks went into the tallow, then hung it back on the poles. A wooden tray beneath caught the tallow that dripped. By the time all the rods of wicks had been dipped, the first were cool enough to dip again. Over and over, the wicks went into the tallow until Prue said, "There. They are the right size. You have done well, child."

Prudence like making bayberry candles even better, for it meant picking the gray-white waxy berries in September, watching them boil in a kettle of water sometime in October, and learning to skim off the wax that floated to the top. Bayberry wax made beautiful green candles that smelled so good! Many were shipped to England and other European countries to be sold and bring needed money to the settlers.

Like her brother, Prudence loved the outdoors. When household tasks allowed time off, she and her mother often took long walks but were careful not to stray far

"YOU HAVE DONE WELL, CHILD."

from the settlement unless with Jamie and James. In their long-sleeved gray dresses with snowy collars, cuffs, aprons, and little caps, they looked more alike than ever.

On sunny days, Prue and her daughter took off their shoes while no one was around to watch and wiggled their bare, white toes in the cool grass.

"If only we could be happy like this always," Prudence sighed. Her mother smiled, knowing even the brightest skies could be overcome with dark clouds at any time.

"IF ONLY WE COULD BE HAPPY LIKE THIS ALWAYS."

THE FISHING BOAT ROSE AND FELL WITH THE WAVES.

# 9

# *A Raging Sea*

Ten-year-old James Lowe stared into the sky. How could it have changed so suddenly? Even Father, with all his knowledge of the weather, had not known a storm was coming. The two had set out in their fishing boat just after dawn, determined to bring in a good catch. Soon, winter weather would limit the number of days they could go far enough out to find the best fishing.

"Well, son, it looks like we're in for a squall." Jamie dropped a strong hand to his son's shoulder. "We'd best be heading toward shore. Step lively, lad."

James sprang to obey, thankful for the added strength his last year's growth had given him. Sails billowed like creatures gone crazy in the rising wind. The fishing boat rose and fell with the waves, higher every moment. Strangely enough, he had no fear. Everyone on Plymouth Plantation knew Jamie Lowe was the best fisherman of all. No treacherous storm could sink his boat!

James thought of what Father and Mother had taught him about God, the Heavenly Father. Jesus hadn't been afraid in a storm, either. He had known His Father was in control. The boy took in great gulps of the salty air and looked in the direction they must go to seek shelter. Mountains of white-topped huge waves hid all traces of shore.

"God be praised we have the wind in our favor," Jamie shouted. His powerful hands busied themselves with the task of using the wind to send them shoreward yet still being in control.

James hadn't realized how far out they had come. Now, their boat pitched and tossed, even with Father's and his best efforts. Would they never reach safe harbour? He breathed a sigh of relief when he caught a glimpse of land through the driving rain that pelted. Faster, faster, until—

"James, lad, help me here!"

"JAMES, LAD, HELP ME HERE!"

He leaped toward his father who struggled with the tiller. The ship heeled and a wave battered so hard, the sure-footed boy lost his balance for a single, terrible second. An avalanche of water poured over him carrying him toward the rail!

"God, help my son!" Jamie's roar sounded above the pounding in James' ears. He clutched for the railing—and missed. In another moment, he'd be overboard and no human could live in the raging sea. Mouth filled with water, only his mind could echo his father's prayer.

A heartbeat later, the ship swung back the other way, carrying James with it. Helpless before the force of the wave, he knew when the fishing boat again heeled, he'd be swept into the ocean. He tried to dig in his boot toes and clutched for anything to hold him but failed. Despair filled him. Was the sea he loved so well to claim him?

Another monstrous wave loomed, attacked. James started to slide, knowing it was the end. Then fingers of steel gripped his outflung arm, biting through the home-

FINGERS OF STEEL GRIPPED HIS ARM.

spun shirt he wore until he could have screamed with pain. Water washed over him. Those relentless fingers tightened even more, and when the boat tilted back, they yanked James to his feet and into the circle of his father's arm. The boy stood circled from behind while Jamie desperately worked the tiller.

It took a minute to realize that he had not been flung into certain death, but James was no sniveling baby. His hands shot out and joined his father's. Together, they fought the storm.

What felt like a lifetime later, they reached an unknown cove. With a mighty rush the fishing boat slid inside the sheltered waters where the fury of the storm had less power. As sometimes happened, the squall moved on in search of other victims, the ocean's greedy, sucking waves cheated of their prey by a strong father, and a merciful, all-powerful Heavenly Father.

Still, the two fishermen were not out of danger. They must strip, rub their bodies until they glowed with warmth and lost the icy chill from the overpowering

THE FISHING BOAT SLID INTO SHELTERED WATERS.

waves, then put on dry clothing. James' teeth chattered, and never had anything felt better than the long woolen stockings, baggy leather breeches, and double-thick cloth doublet,* all made by his mother and sister.

Gradually, the shaking caused by danger as well as cold stilled. "Father—" James wanted to thank him but the words hid inside his throat and wouldn't come out.

"It is well, lad. We must give thanks to the One who heard our prayers." Together, father and son knelt on the still-wet deck and praised God.

Now that the storm had done its worst and made way for blue skies and the gentlest of breezes, James and Jamie decided to go ashore and explore the unfamiliar cove. "'Tis strange in all the time I've fished, I haven't run across this bit of land," Jamie said. "Perhaps because we usually go farther out. Come. Let us see what is here."

"We were blown off course, weren't we, Father?" James curiously looked around him. The dark forest

*jacket

"WE WERE BLOWN OFF COURSE, WEREN'T WE, FATHER?"

felt strange, unlike those near Plymouth. What dangers might lurk in its depths? Never cowardly, still he hesitated, unwilling to go exploring.

Not so his father. Jamie Lowe had never gotten over his desire for adventure. The looming forest and new trails beckoned like a clear call to see what lay in their depths. With sure step and face more eager than his son, he led the way.

At first, everything resembled other forests, James found with relief. Singing birds and tall trees. Rotted stumps from dead trees struck by lightning. Moss and grass in open areas. A tiny stream limping its slow way to the sea.

"If ever a man gets to feeling too crowded on Plymouth Plantation, he could build here," Jamie said.

"What about Indians?" The instant he asked, James wished he hadn't. Again, a sense of trouble rested on him.

"One day red man and white will live in peace," his father told him. "They must, or both will die." He sighed

"... HE COULD BUILD HERE."

and a look of longing crept into his dark eyes. "Son, we have been blessed. If our Father hadn't sent Samoset and Squanto to us..." He never finished the sentence. With a loud cry, an almost-naked Indian hurled himself from behind a large tree directly at him.

"Run, James!" Jamie shouted when a second fell on him and knocked him to the ground, musket flying.

Fear put wings to his study boots. All the races James had run with his friends at the settlement gave him a fleetness of foot. Long hours in the forest with his father provided skill and tricks Squanto had once taught the older man. Knowledge that he must get help drove him to his best. Using every ounce of cunning, he ran until his heart felt it would burst, only glancing back once to see both Indians busy with his father.

"Don't waste time looking over your shoulder if you're ever running for your life," Father had warned. Now, like a firm hand on his arm, all the teachings came to him. James slowed, turned his face in the direction Plymouth Plantation must lie, then bowed his head and

"RUN, JAMES!"

prayed, "Please, help me, and take care of Father."

The little stream offered a good opportunity to hide his tracks in case the Indians trailed him. He waded in and followed it until it became a trickle, then instead of stepping to the bank and leaving footprints, he leaped for a cluster of overhanging branches and swung into a nearby tree. Gritting his teeth and grabbing for the branches of other trees that had grown together into a lacy green canopy, he traveled for a long way from tree to tree.

At last, he dared come down. Now, how could he get across the big clearing in front of him?

He must. "What would Father do?" he wondered. A grin chased some of the worry from his face. He slipped from his doublet and tore pieces from it with hands made strong and sure by knotting rope and hoisting sails on the fishing boat. Next he took off his boots, wrapped the heavy cloth around and around his feet, and tied the pieces on top. "There! No Indian dog can get my scent," he rejoiced. Again, he set off toward home, knowing

" WHAT WOULD FATHER DO ? "

weary miles lay between him and the help Father needed so badly.

At first, he made good time but as the afternoon fled, and with it daylight, James slowed. The battering his body had received during the storm had drained some of his strength. So had lack of food. What he wouldn't give for a chunk of Mother's corn bread and a glass of sweet milk! His mouth watered, and he looked around for food. The berries were long since gone. Squirrels had stripped the nuts and hidden them away. A lop-sided moon slid into the darkening sky and peered down at the hungry boy. Dark shadows surrounded him, and he sang all the hymns he could remember to chase away fear, but barely above a whisper in case unfriendly ears listened in the night.

Stumbling with weariness, he yawned, and fought sleep until he could go no more. James muttered, "Have to rest, just a moment." By the pale moonlight he chose a large tree for his resting place, climbed high into the branches, wedged himself into a natural seat formed by

DARK SHADOWS SURROUNDED HIM.

twisted limbs, and fell asleep.

Minutes or hours later, he woke to the sound of many voices and torches. He opened his mouth to cry out for gladness. Surely, Governor Bradford had sent out a rescue party when Jamie and his son had failed to come home. Mother would have reported their absence at dusk. A warning voice inside whispered, *Don't speak.*

James clamped his mouth shut and gently parted the branches so he could see. Cold fear worse than when he'd known he'd be thrown into the sea raced through his wiry body. He clamped a hand over his mouth to keep from making noise that would give away his hiding place.

Far below his tree, torch light shone on a dozen bronzed faces. This was no rescue party but a band of Indians abroad in the night.

THIS WAS NO RESCUE PARTY.

"MASSASOIT!"

# 10
## *No One to Help but God*

Only James' death grip around the tree trunk kept him from tumbling down onto the Indians. For a moment, he felt fear in the pit of his stomach until he wondered if he could hang on. It made him sick and weak. *What would Father do?* he silently asked himself. The next instant a single word flashed to his mind: *pray*.

"There's no one to help but You, God," James whispered, so low he knew only God could hear. "If the Indians take me, too, what will happen to Father?"

Loud chatter and laughter from below interrupted his prayer. Again, he peered down through the branches. A tall Indian stood with torch upheld. It lighted his solemn face. Relief ran through the watching boy like a river in flood. "Massasoit!"

The chief dropped his torch and whipped around, in

time to catch James when he slid down the tree trunk. Dark eyes peered suspiciously at his captive and into the tree branches.

James shook his head, so thankful to God he waved his arms up and down. "Two Indians jumped Father. We were driven ashore by the storm." His hands painted the story in the air until the Indians grunted and in a combination of English and Indian language showed they understood and would help him.

James never forgot the long trip back to where he had parted from his father. Too proud to complain of weariness, he took strength from hope and from the dried meat Massasoit gave him  Even when his legs felt they could not move one more step, he went on until they reached the exact spot of the struggle. Disappointment filled him. Only torn grass and disturbed ground showed signs of the struggle.

He bit his lip to keep back tears, a sign of weakness the Indians would despise. Massasoit waved his hand, and his braves made camp. James knew he wouldn't

"TWO INDIANS JUMPED FATHER."

sleep at all, but his tired body and mind couldn't keep going.

He awoke to sunny skies and leaped up, ready to track his father. "I wonder why Massasoit is smiling?" he wondered to himself as he hungrily ate the food given to him. The next minute he knew. A group of men, two with bound hands, prodded by some of Massasoit's men, stumbled into the clearing—and a tall, beaming white man walked after them.

"Father!" Breakfast forgotten, James ran to the little band. "I thought you were—"

"Takes more than two Indians to get me," Jamie chuckled. "Can't say what would have happened, though, if they had taken me to the tribe, as they'd planned." He smiled and his hand shot out to Massasoit. "Peace, and I thank you." The chief shook hands and bowed.

Instead of going overland, Jamie decided he and James would sail back on their fishing boat, using the breeze that had sprung up to the best advantage. Massasoit told them he and his braves would take the

"FATHER!"

two Indians to their tribe and warn them about capturing white men.

Several hours later the fishermen reached Plymouth Plantation. Prue and Prudence met them at the water's edge. "We thought the storm had swallowed you," they cried.

"It almost did," James burst out. "Then the Indians jumped on Father and I ran and—" An ocean of words poured out. "Massasoit came, and we're safe, Mother," he finished. "But oh, I am so hungry!"

Later when he lay sleeping, Prue looked into his young face and thanked God. She thought how all her life she had heard women say, "Men go to sea and to war while women wait." Sometimes she thought the waiting must be the hardest part. Yet, she wouldn't change Jamie. He had chosen his path and James after him. All she and her daughter could do was join the army of those who waited—and prayed.

❖

The years continued to pass, some the same as oth-

PRUE THANKED GOD.

ers, many marked by new happenings. Wicked men stirred up trouble with the Indians, sometimes making promises and not keeping them, taking their beaver skins and giving them little in return. Sickness visited the plantation and had to be fought by those who remained healthy. Prue taught her small daughter well, and Prudence Lowe became a fine nurse, much in demand by those with loved ones who fell ill.

More and more villages sprang up, farming settlements built in the same general pattern. Once Prudence told James, after a visit to friends in a different village, "It's so like Plymouth Plantation it is as if we hadn't gone anywhere else!"

He laughed, the same way his father once had laughed at their mother in Holland. His dark eyes twinkled. "There's the village green in the middle, with the cows munching grass, the village cow pasture back of the houses grouped around the green."

Prudence took up the story, a wide smile on her face. "The general store and blacksmith shop and tavern, grist-

HIS DARK EYES TWINKLED.

mill and schoolhouse. The meetinghouse and the minister's home."

"Horses kicking up dust on the dirt road." He pointed. "Prudence, did you hear about the last town meeting? Father said the schoolmaster should be paid more."

"He should." Her head bobbed up and down. "He is kind and doesn't punish us for laughing if something is funny."

The comparing game ended when James whooped, "Here comes the postrider. Let's see if we have any mail." They hurried to where the man on horseback who carried mail from town to town had just reined in his mount. Today, he carried nothing for the Lowes but brought news of trouble brewing with the Dutch and Indians. Even worse, sickness had fallen on both of these groups.

"Father, Governor Bradford says it pleased the Lord to visit those people with illness," Prudence said one evening. "Many of the Indians are sick, too. Does God only love the English?"

"DOES GOD ONLY LOVE THE ENGLISH?"

Her father and mother looked at one another before Jamie quietly said, "We don't hold with that idea." He pressed his lips tight together. "Remember a time back when the swarms of flies as big as bumblebees* came out of holes in the ground? They ate all the green things and made such a noise the woods rang. The Indians said sickness would follow, as it has during the hot summer months."

"Why do you still call him Governor Bradford?" James teased. "Edward Winslow and Thomas Prence have been voted in."

"Governor Bradford will be in office again," Prudence told him. "He was for years and will be chosen by the men when they vote." Her prediction proved right. William Bradford served as governor every year between 1621 and 1657 except for five.

New trouble came in the form of a smallpox epidemic among the Indians that killed many in spite of all the nursing help the English settlers kindly gave them when

---

*seventeen-year locusts

"WE DON'T HOLD WITH THAT IDEA."

the Indians grew so sick they could not care for their own. Prue marveled that not one of her people who stepped into the horrible situation and did what they could fell ill of smallpox. As had happened before, the goodwill and efforts of those who nursed the Indians did much to restore kindly feelings toward the English among the Indians.

More trouble began with the coming of the French who wanted to take possession in the name of the king of France. They also supplied arms to the Indians and added to the danger. Stories drifted to Plymouth Plantation of terror in other parts of the country. Roving Indian bands attacked settlers, both men and women, working in the fields. They even tried to take a fort, but failed. Although Plymouth itself remained safe, heartache for those so persecuted touched the Lowe family and many others. Some Indian tribes who had long been enemies, now joined in peace against the English, who they saw as their common foe, then turned around and came back to help the settlers when things didn't go

THEY TRIED TO TAKE A FORT, BUT FAILED.

well.

Both sides were guilty of killing and Jamie privately told Prue, "It sickens me to hear our leaders praising God for being able to kill four hundred Indians in one day! Sometimes I wonder if we are any better than they." Yet he dared not say any such thing outside his own family for fear of punishment. He believed it right to defend themselves from attack, but all the shedding of blood made him wish more than ever before for lasting peace.

❖

June, 1638, arrived with a fearful earthquake that rumbled and violently flung dishes from their shelves. Prue and Prudence ran outdoors and gasped. They clutched the doorposts in order to keep from being thrown to the ground while the earth trembled beneath their feet. Not only did the seacoast shudder, but Jamie and James, in their fishing boat, were shaken as well.

Connecticut and New Haven continued to be plagued by Indian troubles, sometimes getting caught between

JUNE, 1638, ARRIVED WITH A FEARFUL EARTHQUAKE.

hostile tribes who appealed to the English for help against their enemies. War clouds hovered overhead. Yet various treaties prevented war, at least for a time.

❖

In 1646, Prudence of Plymouth Plantation, proudly counted her blessings, grandchildren gathered around her. Silver threads brightened her flaxen hair and shone in Jamie's dark, tousled mane. The love in his eyes shone as brightly as the day more than 25 years earlier when he had crept up behind her while she'd hung up clothes in Holland.

The years had been long and sometimes hard, she thought. Yet, if she could, would she have chosen differently?

Prue looked at Prudence and her young husband who gazed into their new baby's face. She turned her head toward sturdy James, playing with his sons who already showed signs of following in the family fishing business. No. She wouldn't trade places with anyone.

"Grandmother, tell us about the *Mayflower*," small

THE YEARS HAD BEEN LONG AND SOMETIMES HARD.

d. "Why did you leave your home and
erica?"

ed into the eager faces. "So we could wor-
and make a land for our families to be true,"
. "Governor Bradford once said, '...As one small
may light a thousand, so the light here kindled
hone unto many, yes, in some sense to our whole
on.'"

"I don't know what that means," a grandchild complained.

Prue looked at her circle of loved ones and smiled.
"Someday," she promised, "you will."

"SOMEDAY... YOU WILL."

CHRISTOPHER
COLUMBUS

AT A CHRISTIAN BOOKSTORE NEAR

# Awesome Books for Kids!

## Young Reader's Christian Library
## Action, Adventure, and Fun Reading!

This series for young readers ages 8 to 15 is action-packed, fast-paced, and Christ-centered! With exciting illustrations on every other page following the text, kids won't be able to put these books down! Over 100 illustrations per book. All books are paperbound. The unique size (4-3/16" X 5-3/8") makes these books easy to take anywhere!

   **A Selection to Satisfy All Kids!**

Abraham Lincoln
At the Back of the North Wind
Ben-Hur
Christopher Columbus
Corrie ten Boom
David Livingstone
Dark Secret of the Ouija, The
Elijah
Heidi
Hudson Taylor
In His Steps
Jesus

Joseph
Miriam
Paul
Peter
Pilgrim's Progress, The
Prudence of Plymouth
        Planation
Robinson Crusoe
Ruth
Samuel Morris
Swiss Family Robinson, The
Thunder in the Valley
Wagons West